WOMEN IN WHITE (CUBA)

MISTLETOE (SCANDINAVIA)

CRANE (JAPAN)

WHITE POPPY (BRITISH COMMONWEALTH)

GRASS (EASTERN AFRICA)

YIN/YANG (CHINA)

Let There Be

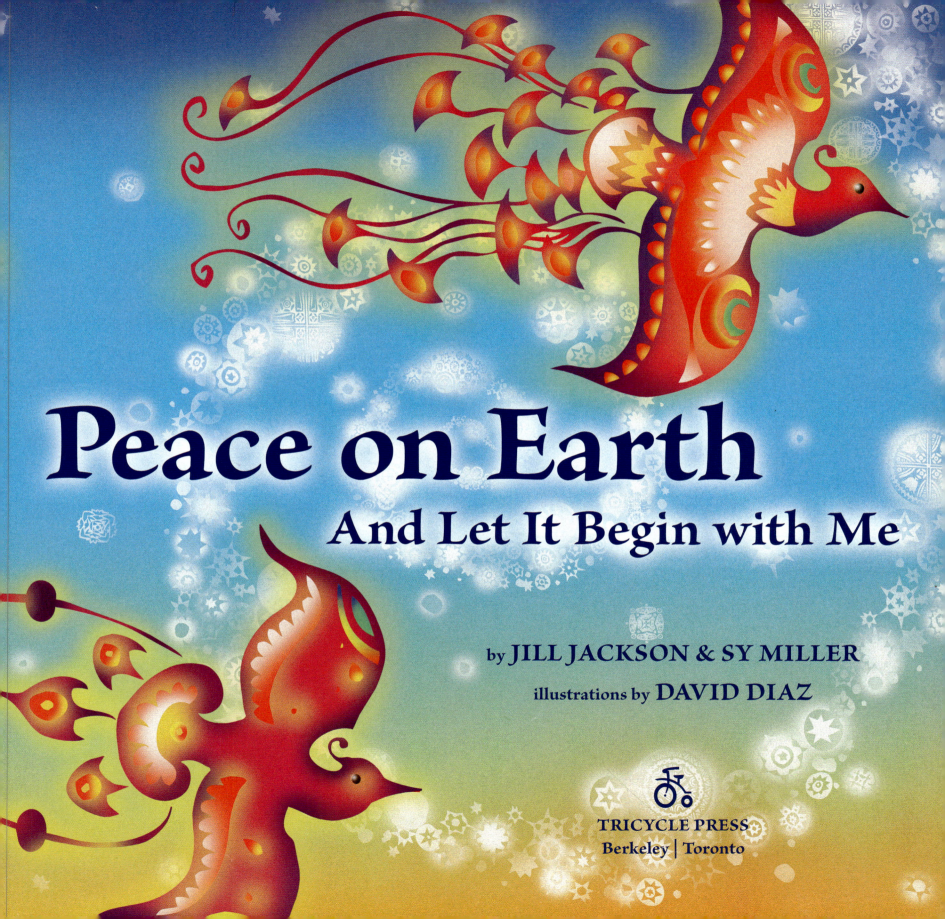

Peace on Earth
And Let It Begin with Me

by JILL JACKSON & SY MILLER

illustrations by DAVID DIAZ

TRICYCLE PRESS
Berkeley | Toronto

Let there be
peace on earth...

and let it begin
with me.

Let there be peace on earth,

the peace that was meant to be.

With God as our Father, brothers all are we.

(alt) With Earth as our Mother, family all are we.

Let me walk with my brother
in perfect harmony.

Let peace begin with me—

let this be the moment now.

With every step I take,

let this be my   solemn vow:

To take each moment
and live each moment
in peace eternally.

Let there
be peace on
earth

and let
it begin
with me.

ABOUT THE SONGWRITERS

Sy Miller was born in 1908 in Brooklyn, New York. As a little boy, he was given piano lessons and first discovered his love for music. After he grew up and served in the Army, Sy began a career in music, writing in Hollywood with the Warner Brothers Music Department. There he composed songs and special material for films and television shows such as *The Andy Williams Show* and *Hawaii Five-O*. He also wrote many songs independently and worked as a singing coach.

Jill Jackson was born in Independence, Missouri, in 1913. Her mother died when she was very young and Jill became a ward of the court and was put into foster care. During these lonely years she felt most at home in nature, where she felt accepted just as she was.

As a young woman, Jill went to Hollywood and worked as an actress in western films of the 1930s. Years later, after she had married and become a mother, Jill began writing songs for children with her husband and collaborator, Sy Miller. Jill wrote the lyrics, and Sy wrote the melodies to their songs.

HOW THE SONG CAME TO BE

One morning, after Jill had been writing songs with Sy for some years, she awoke with the words, "Let there be peace on earth and let it begin with me," running through her head.

The thought amazed her—"Let it begin with *with me!*" She realized in that moment that every one of us can create peace. No need to wait, hoping for someone to give it to us. No matter who we are, we can make peace happen beginning right now, this very moment.

Wanting to share the idea, Jill got up, went to her desk and began to write the words to a new song. Sy, working with her, wrote the melody. "Let There Be Peace on Earth" came from both of their hearts.

Perhaps the idea for the song had been born from the yearning of a troubled child for peace, or from having lived through wars and fears of nuclear bombs, or from having read about families torn apart by conflicts. Jill had always yearned for peace in her own life and peace for every person in the world. However, she herself would tell you that the idea for "Let There Be Peace on Earth" had come through her, and not from her.

HOW THE SONG TOOK WINGS

"One summer evening in 1955, a group of 180 teenagers of different races and religions, meeting at a workshop high in the California mountains, locked arms, formed a circle, and sang a song of peace. They believed that singing the song with its simple, basic sentiment—'Let There Be Peace on Earth and Let it Begin with Me'—would help to create a climate for world peace and understanding." —Sy Miller

In time, the song spread to all fifty states and was sung at graduations, meetings, holiday gatherings, and services. It became a theme for Veteran's Day and Human Rights Day. The United Auto Workers and 4-H Clubs sang it.

Many artists recorded and performed the song, among them Nat King Cole, Vince Gill, Patti Page, Bing Crosby, Mahalia Jackson, Pearl Bailey, Gladys Knight and the Pips, and The Boston Pops Orchestra. It won the Valley Forge Freedom Foundation's George Washington Medal and the Brotherhood Award from the National Conference of Christians and Jews.

"Let There Be Peace on Earth" was performed for presidents, dignitaries, and heads of state, including the Pope; Presidents Carter, Reagan, and Clinton; and Nikita Khrushchev.

The song traveled overseas, eventually spreading to all of the continents. The Maoris in New Zealand sang it. The Zulus in South Africa sang it. It was used as a theme by the United Nations and by UNICEF.

Together Sy and Jill raised two daughters and wrote more than seventy songs—songs for children, lullabies, inspirational pieces, and ballads. From the piano in the corner of the living room, Sy's music often filled the house. He and Jill lived a happy life together. In 1971, Sy passed away, leaving his wife, children, and grandchildren to miss him deeply.

In the later part of Jill's life, she continued to share the message of "Let There Be Peace on Earth," giving talks all over the country on peace, personal empowerment, and letting it "begin with me." The idea endlessly inspired her, and she loved sharing it.

Jill passed away peacefully in her home in 1995. Today Sy and Jill's work lives on, perpetuated by the many people who share their vision of peace for every man, woman, and child on earth.

SONGS ON THE CD

Sy and Jill wrote all of the songs on the CD, except for "Golden Rule," which was written by their daughter, Jan Tache. The musical group Palo Colorado recorded the songs. Friends and family members sang on the CD with Palo Colorado, including Jill and Sy's great-grandchildren, Emily and Joe. We are delighted to present this music to you and hope that you will enjoy all of the songs.

1. Let There Be Peace on Earth (And Let It Begin with Me)—Vocals: Seymour Liberty
2. Hoopety-Hey Kind Of Day—Vocals: Kemba Russell, Yoko Imai, Joe Mann
3. Everything Is Important to Life—Vocals: Mayteana Morales
4. Take a Moment—Vocals: Nico Georis, Kemba Russell, Robin MacMillan
5. Golden Rule—Vocals: Nico Georis, Jacob Silver and several chickens
6. I Love the Outdoors—Vocals: Kemba Russell
7. French Interlude—Vocals: Choir
8. It's Up to You and Me—Vocals: Nico Georis, Makiah Epstein, Jacob Silver, Emily Mann
9. Keep in Touch—Vocals: Makiah Epstein
10. Still Small Voice—Vocals: Nico Georis, Jacob Silver, Mayteana Morales
11. Wonderful Child—Vocals: Nico Georis, Jacob Silver, Kemba Russell, Mayteana Morales
12. Let There Be Peace on Earth (And Let It Begin with Me)—Instrumental

Palo Colorado

Nico Georis—Piano, prepared and electric pianos, organs, clavinet, acoustic guitar, percussion

Jacob Silver—Electric bass, double bass, electric and acoustic guitars, percussion

Robin MacMillan—Drums and percussion

Palo Colorado is the sound of six romping feet and thirty flying fingers that enjoy nothing more than spinning music for the hearts and ears of all. Jacob Silver, Robin MacMillan, and Nico Georis have been playing music together since they were but wee lads, growing up along the coast of California. They have since relocated to Brooklyn, New York, where they live and play in their recording studio, Media Blitz East.

Additional Musicians

Pico Alt—Violin
Jason Colby—Trumpet
Christina Courtin—Viola
Oran Etkan—Clarinet, bass clarinet, tenor saxophone
Stafford Hunter—Trombone
Jane O'Hara—Cello
Ryan Scot—Pedal steel
Yusuke Yamamoto—Flute

Choir

Makiah Epstein, Bill Ford, Jeanne Ford, Gaston Georis, Nico Georis, Sheila Georis, Robin MacMillan, Emily Mann, Joe Mann, Anita Silver, Jacob Silver.

Engineered by Drew Fischer at Media Blitz East in Brooklyn, New York, and Prairie Sun Studios in Cotati, California.

Mixed by Drew Fischer and Palo Colorado.

Arrangements and orchestration by Nico Georis and Palo Colorado.

Music produced by Jan-Lee Music and Palo Colorado.

Mastered by Mark Christensen at Engine Room Audio.

www.lettherebepeacecd.com

LET THERE BE PEACE ON EARTH

SY MILLER and JILL JACKSON

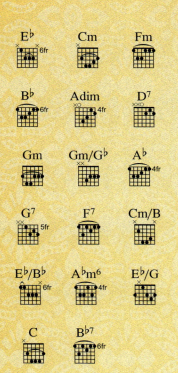

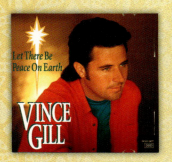

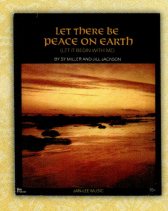

ABOUT THE PEACE SYMBOLS

Throughout history, cultures around the world have used an array of symbols to communicate their desire for peace. Below are just a few of these. Each can be found somewhere in this book—see if you can spot all of them!

Mistletoe (Scandinavia): In ancient times, adversaries would stand together beneath a spray of mistletoe to make a peace compact. Sometimes the peace would be sealed with a kiss, thus our modern-day tradition of kissing under the mistletoe!

Grass (Eastern Africa): Grass has a sacred importance to the Masai, a tribe in eastern Africa, because it feeds the cattle that are crucial to the tribe's survival. A tuft of grass is held in the right hand as a sign of peace and is used for blessings during rituals.

Loon (Pacific Northwestern America): To many of the native peoples of the Pacific Northwest, the loon symbolizes peace, tranquility, and generosity. With its haunting call, the loon was thought to have the power to awaken one's deepest hopes and dreams.

Dove (Universal): Many of the ancient texts tell the story of a dove that carried an olive branch and heralded land after a great flood. Mythologies and stories from places as far ranging as ancient Egypt, India, the Middle East, Azerbaijan, Russia, and the Americas also feature doves as representatives of peace.

Palm Tree (Middle East): In many historical cultures, palm trees were symbols of peace, prosperity, and fertility. The date palm may well be one of the oldest cultivated food-producing plants.

The Women in White (Cuba): The Women in White gather every Sunday to peacefully protest the imprisonment of their husbands and sons for political dissidence.

Yin and Yang (China): The yin/yang symbol is fundamental to traditional Chinese philosophy, which states that everything in the universe is essentially the union of two opposing forces: dark and light, cold and hot, male and female. These two forces are called yin and yang. The yin/yang circle shows those two forces in perfect harmony, each interdependent and creating a balanced whole.

White Poppy (British Commonwealth): A British organization called the Peace Pledge Union began distributing white poppies in 1934 "as a pledge…that war must not happen again." Today, the symbol is recognized throughout the British Commonwealth as a way to remember the victims of war without glorifying militarism.

Doe (Tibet): In traditional Tibetan culture, the doe symbolizes harmony and peace. Tibetan tales tell of deer so compassionate that they are driven to intercede in human conflict, risking their own lives in the process.

Turtle (South Pacific): The Hawaiian word for Earth, *Honua*, is close to *honu*, the word for turtle. The *honu*, or South Pacific green sea turtle, is a symbol of peace, humility, and the spirit within. Hawaiian mythology tells of a turtle that could turn itself into a little girl to play with and protect the children of the island.

Crane (Japan): A Japanese legend says that anyone who folds a thousand paper cranes would be granted a wish. In the early 1950s, twelve-year-old Sadako Sasaki was diagnosed with leukemia caused by radiation from the bombing of Hiroshima. Sadako determined that she would fold one thousand cranes in the hopes of fulfilling her wish for health, happiness, and peace. Though Sadako died of the illness, she succeeded in transforming the crane into a symbol of peace for children all over the world.

Lion and Lamb (Mediterranean): This symbol refers to the idea and hope that all will live in peace together—the weak and the powerful, the hunter and the hunted, the feared and the fearful, and the lion and the lamb.

To Jill and Sy, who were able to put the dream into a song. With gratitude and love.
—J. T. & J. F.

For lil' Elvis —D. D.

We gratefully acknowledge the following people: Tricycle Press for the depth of their vision; David Diaz for his magical paintings; Palo Colorado, the singers, and musicians for their creative genius; Magnus Toren and the Henry Miller Library for advice and encouragement; Shawna Garritson for her enthusiasm; Dave and Sherry Pettus and the Stephen B. Hard Foundation for their generous support; Sara Thomsen for her beautiful voice; Don Ackland for carrying the torch; Lisa Kleissner for exercising the power of six; and our loving families for being themselves.

—Jan Tache and Jeannie Ford
Daughter and Granddaughter of Sy and Jill Miller

TRICYCLE PRESS
an imprint of Ten Speed Press
PO Box 7123
Berkeley, California 94707
www.tricyclepress.com

Design by Katy Brown
Typeset in Brioso and Adobe Caslon
The illustrations in this book were rendered in Adobe Illustrator and Photoshop
Picture Credits: Dora Hall album cover courtesy of Robert Hulseman;
Vince Gill album cover courtesy MCA Nashville; "Winged Dove" by
Milton Glaser, courtesy Milton Glaser Collection, Milton Glaser Design
Study Center, and Archives Visual Arts Foundation (Milton Glaser is the
designer and copyright holder of this piece); "Let There Be Peace on Earth"
sheet music courtesy Jan-Lee Music.

Library of Congress Cataloging-in-Publication Data

Jackson, Jill.
Let there be peace on earth : and let it begin with me /
by Jill Jackson & Sy Miller.
    p. cm.
    Summary: Illustrates the award-winning song about each person's
responsibility to help bring about world peace. Includes a history of the song
and biographical notes on the husband and wife songwriting team.
    ISBN-13: 978-1-58246-285-1 (hardcover)
    ISBN-10: 1-58246-285-2 (hardcover)
    1. Children's songs—Texts. [1. Peace—Songs and music. 2. Songs.]
I. Miller, Sy. II. Title.
    PZ8.3.J13483Let 2009
    782.42164'0268—dc22
    [E]
                           2008043122
First Tricycle Press printing, 2009
Printed in China

1 2 3 4 5 6 — 13 12 11 10 09

NOV   2009